NICK JR.

DORA the **EXPLORER**®

Super Babies!

adapted by Alison Inches
based on the original teleplay by Leslie Valdes
illustrated by Victoria Miller

Simon Spotlight/Nick Jr.
New York   London   Toronto   Sydney

Based on the TV series *Dora the Explorer*® as seen on Nick Jr.®

SIMON SPOTLIGHT
An imprint of Simon & Schuster Children's Publishing Division
1230 Avenue of the Americas, New York, New York 10020
© 2006 Viacom International Inc. All rights reserved.
NICK JR., *Dora the Explorer*, and all related titles, logos, and characters are
registered trademarks of Viacom International Inc.
All rights reserved, including the right of reproduction in whole or in part in any form.
SIMON SPOTLIGHT and colophon are registered trademarks of Simon & Schuster, Inc.
Manufactured in the United States of America
8 10 9 7
ISBN-13: 978-1-4169-1485-3
ISBN-10: 1-4169-1485-4

¡Hola! I'm Dora. Boots and I are feeding my baby brother and sister their Banana Baby Food. They love bananas—just like Boots! They also love it when I tell them stories. Do you want to hear the Super Babies story? Great!

Once upon a time there lived twin babies—a boy and a girl. They were Super Babies!

The Super Babies could Super Fly!

They could Super Crawl!

They could Super Cry!

They were
Super Strong!

And most of all, they loved their Super Banana Baby Food.

One day a sneaky fox named Swiper started swiping everyone's bananas. He even swiped the Super Babies' Banana Baby Food!

Swiper threw all the bananas far, far away.
"You'll never find your bananas now!" said Swiper, laughing.

The Super Babies wanted to get their Baby Banana Food back! To get to the bananas, Map said that we had to go through the Bubble Bath and climb up the Building Blocks. And that's how we'd get to the bananas!

The Super Babies got into their Super Stroller, and off we zoomed! *Goo-goo, gaa-gaa!*

First we needed to find the Bubble Bath. The Super Babies used their Super Hearing to hear the bubbles all the way down the road! *Pop, pop, pop!*

But when we tried to follow the road, we found something blocking it—a Big, Blue Baby Bear who was sound asleep!

To wake up the Big, Blue Baby Bear, the Super Babies had to Super Cry. We helped them! *Wahhh! Wahhh!*

The Super Crying worked! The Big, Blue Baby Bear woke up and stepped out of the way so we could make it to the Bubble Bath.

But how would we get across?

The Super Babies knew the answer: They would use their Super Blowing to blow up a boat so we could paddle across!

There were so many bubbles in the Bubble Bath—and they were really big! *¡Burbujas súper grandes!* We needed to Super Pop the bubbles with our fingers. *Pop! Pop! Pop!*

After crossing the Bubble Bath, we needed to find the Building Blocks. But we couldn't see them! So the Super Babies used their Super X-ray Vision to see the Building Blocks through a rock!

When we got to the Building Blocks we had to find a way to get up to the cliff. We needed to use the blocks to make steps! The blocks were too heavy for Boots and me to lift. . . .

Goo-goo, ga-ga!
But the Super Babies could do it! They Super Lifted the Building Blocks and made five Super Steps!

We counted in Spanish as we climbed to the top: *¡Uno, dos, tres, cuatro, cinco!*

We made it over the Building Blocks! But where were the bananas? The Super Babies used their Super Strength to lift us higher and higher . . . until we could see the bananas!

The Super Babies then had to Super Fly us to the bananas! But soon the Super Babies got tired. They were thirsty! We needed some bottles! *¡Los biberones!* Where could we get some bottles?

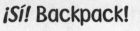

¡Sí! Backpack!

Luckily Backpack had some bottles for the Super Babies.
After having a Super Drink, the Super Babies were ready to
take off again!

The Super Babies flew us all the way to the bananas and their Banana Baby Food! There were bananas everywhere. There was even a walking banana! But wait—bananas don't walk. . . .

It wasn't a *banana*—it was Swiper!

Swiper was going to swipe the Super Babies' Banana Baby Food again! We had to say "Swiper, no swiping!"

It worked! The Babies were finally able to eat their Banana Baby Food. *¡Lo hicimos!* We did it!

Hooray! We had a great time telling the Super Babies story. What was your Super Favorite part?